AuthorHouse™
1663 Liberty Drive
Bloomington, IN 47403
www.authorhouse.com
Phone: 1-800-839-8640

Published by AuthorHouse 04/22/2013

ISBN: 978-1-4817-0829-6 (sc)
978-1-4817-0830-2 (e)

Library of Congress Control Number: 2013900932

Whistle Warriors

Erik Roberts and Marcia Walker
Illustrated by Susan Shorter

authorHOUSE®

WHISTLE WARRIORS

Erik Roberts and Marcia Walker

Illustrated by Susan Shorter

PART ONE

The last bell rang! All the kids at Frederick Douglas Elementary in northern Prince Georges Maryland were excited. The beginning of summer break was finally here!

This summer would be especially great, because the kids from my neighborhood on Cypress Street were going to an adventure camp off the Susquehanna River four hours away in Pennsylvania. That included my kid brother Alante who is a year younger than me and in the third grade, his friends Shelly Simmons and Laura Johnson, my best friend Henry Milton who I have been friends with since first grade, and me.

Here's a crazy story about my friendship with Henry. When we first met, we didn't even like each other. You could say Henry was a bully back then.

I remember our first grade teacher, Ms. Morales, introducing me on my first day of school. "Class, this is Erik Glen. Please say hello and welcome him."

"Hello, Erik," everyone said, except this one boy who balled up his fist and poked out his tongue.

Just my luck! Ms. Morales sat me right next to this kid who was much taller and tougher looking than me.

"Now, Henry," she said, "you behave and make friends with Erik, because he is going to be your class partner." She walked away, leaving me next to a troublemaker.

"I'm going to kick your butt," he told me.

True to his word, at lunch when Ms. Morales wasn't paying attention, he grabbed me and pushed me off the monkey bars. I sat amazed that this bully wanted to fight a scrawny kid like me. While I was on the ground, I was thinking about what to do, and I remembered my mom and dad saying I should protect myself.

"What are you going to do new boy?" jeered Henry, as my classmates look on.

I stood up and surprised myself by charging right into his belly. And guess what?

I didn't lose. Henry was now the one lying on the ground. The kids laughed and pointed fingers at him.

Ms. Morales finally noticed the scuffle and broke us up. She said we had to apologize to each other. I did, but Henry would not. She called both of our parents.

Great! My first day at a new school and I was already in trouble. I knew this kid would not let it go either, so when I got home, I asked my parents what should I do the next time he wanted to fight.

Mom said, "Make sure you tell the teacher."

Dad said, "We don't start fights, but make sure you protect yourself."

Parents can be so confusing. Do I fight or not?

That night I had a wild dream that a monster was attacking Alante and me from under our beds. We kept running, but he captured us and squeezed us until we burst. We popped like firecrackers. Pop! Pop! Pop! I woke up sweating, and I checked to make sure my little brother was okay.

The next day, I was amazed when Henry came over to me at my desk and apologized. We are now in the fourth grade and we've been friends ever since that day.

Alante met Shelly in Mr. Albert's second-grade class a year ago. Shelly moved next door to us and across the street from her cousin Laura Jackson. I had known Laura from school, but we were not friends. Henry liked Laura. She wasn't too talkative and she preferred reading her books while the rest of us were outside playing. Sometimes, she would ride her bike to the playground where we played basketball. She'd watch us, then she would leave.

I thought she was weird. Henry said she was just super smart. Laura looked like Rudy from *The Cosby Show*, and she had her hair styled like Minnie Mouse, I thought.

When Shelly moved in the neighborhood, Laura started to show her fun side. Shelly and her mom had moved to Maryland from Miami, Florida. She resembled the *That's So Raven* girl. She was a lot like Alante, who enjoyed telling jokes, making up funny stories, and playing basketball. Not bad for a girl.

Shelly and my brother were in the same class, and they became fast friends. Laura started tagging along with them, enjoying their company and crazy stories. Pretty soon, we were all hanging out around the neighborhood together. Laura was great at helping us with our math homework. Henry was right, the girl was super smart.

Alante and I looked very much alike. We could have passed for twins, except I was much taller. I liked my clothes and tennis shoes looking nice all day. Alante would run around all covered with mud and grass stains; he'd wear holey shirts and dirty shoes. That was another thing he liked about Shelly, she didn't care the least bit if she got dirty.

When we got home from school that day, our parents sat us down to talk about the summer camp.

"Boys," Mom said, "your father and I have the list of supplies that you need for your camping trip. "We're all going shopping tonight."

"Erik," Dad said, "you are going with me to get the camping equipment. Alante, you will go with your mom to the Super Center. Matter of fact, Henry's dad will be going along with us too."

"What about Shelly and Laura? Can they go with us?" Alante asked.

"Don't worry, I saw Laura's mom today and she said they will go tomorrow," Mom said. "Now, go play and be back by six."

Henry knocked at our door and we ran outside. Alante went to Laura's house to get Shelly and they biked over to the basketball court. We fooled around playing tag and basketball, then we went up into Henry's tree house and sat telling jokes.

Mom called us at exactly six o'clock.

"What an expensive camp!" Mom said to Miss Essie, Mr. Milton's new wife, as they headed out the door with Alante. The three of them took off in our Toyota for the Super Center near the I-83 highway.

We headed out in Henry's dad's big Suburban. With all the camping equipment on that list, we were happy to have that monster truck available. Our list included:

- ✴ Tents
- ✴ Sleeping bags
- ✴ Sheets
- ✴ Blankets
- ✴ Pillows
- ✴ Hiking gear
- ✴ First-aid supplies
- ✴ Books
- ✴ Magazines
- ✴ Grooming supplies
- ✴ Extra clothing, swimsuits
- ✴ Medications
- ✴ Snacks
- ✴ NO ELECTRONICS

When dad, Mr. Milton, Henry, and I finally arrived in the store, it looked like every family in our neighborhood was there, except Laura's and Shelly's. It was a madhouse!

Three weeks away from home, I mused. All of the parents looked just as excited as the kids.

Henry went off to try on hiking boots as I followed behind my dad and Mr. Milton in the tent aisle. I overheard their conversation about how Shelly's mom was struggling to raise the cash for all the supplies. Dad said she was waiting for Shelly's father to send her some money.

Laura's mom and Shelly's mom are sisters and are of Puerto Rican descent. Shelly's dad Mr. Simmons, is an African American military pilot, and her parents have been separated for two years.

Mrs. Simmons was struggling with her business. Mr. Milton said she was probably going to have to sell her house and move in with Laura's family.

Wow! From the way Shelly played around, laughing all the time, I would never have guessed that her family was breaking apart. I knew all about divorce because Henry's dad divorced his mom five years ago. Henry was sad and became a bully. He talked all the time about missing his mother.

He would see her only once a year because she lost custody. He is still sad about that, but now he plays basketball and runs track to get his aggression out.

Henry quit being a bully in school, but he's still tough and will fight anybody. Often, he would get into scrapes with the fifth graders. The sixth graders would leave us alone for the most part, because they were more interested in going to junior high. Besides, my cousin Eugene and Henry's cousin Lionel were in Mr. Sesay's sixth-grade class and they protected us from the older kids. Although they were helpful, Eugene and Lionel did tease us and boss us around.

Thank goodness the two of them were not going with us to Camp Susquehanna!

Mr. Sesay's graduating class was chosen to go to Africa for the summer by the school board for their work and their donations of safe drinking water in a small African village near Mr. Sesay's hometown of Sierra Leone.

I stopped my musing and went to look for Henry. Before I reached the hiking aisle, someone came up behind me and knocked my cap off my head. It was my cousin Eugene.

"What's up, peep squeak?" he said, rough-housing me a little.

"Leave me alone, Eugene!" I said, trying to shove him away from me.

"Are you going to tell on me?" he jeered. "Besides, I'm just toughening you up."

Just then, Henry and Lionel came around the end of the aisle. They were talking about summer break.

"Come on Eugene, my dad wants us to get some eco-friendly items to take on the safari," Lionel said. "Come on; Leave the kid alone!"

"See you at the end of summer little man," Eugene said.

"He's a jerk!" I said to Henry. "I'm glad he's leaving for junior high. Well, at least you and your cousin are getting along."

"You know, he is not so bad lately," Henry said. "Hey, he even helped me pick out these cool hiking boots."

"I'm still glad they're not coming with us," I said emphatically.

"Me too." echoed Henry.

One week later we were back in front of Frederick Douglas Elementary School. It was noisy, with everyone unloading their cars and families saying their good-byes. Some of the younger kids held tight to their parents, not wanting to leave for the summer. Other kids were running around as the camp counselors tried to get their attention.

The lead camp counselor, Mr. Borzak, said on the megaphone that all of the parents should get their children lined up for the bus. We would be leaving in fifteen minutes. Shelly and Laura still had not arrived.

We were all on the bus, ready to head out. My mom asked Mr. Borzak, "Can you wait a few more minutes for the two other campers?"

"Ma'am, we have a schedule to maintain!" he said. "All parents are aware of the policy. They'll just have to drive up to the Susquehanna Camp site."

Alante was in the back of the bus with a few kids from school, including freckled-faced Jason Beekman and skinny, bucktoothed Timmy Tautlebaum—the third grade class clowns.

Henry and I sat near the entrance of the bus, talking about all the adventures we would soon encounter.

"I'm going rock climbing," Henry said excitedly as the bus door closed and all of the parents waved good-bye.

"I'm going to go water rafting and then swimming," I said, equally excited. The bus continued to roll out.

"Yes, I'm going to swim all day. Alante and his friends want to go hiking and searching for treasures. I hope his friends make it." I said, sneaking an anxious glance at Alante.

"Oh, they will make it all right. Miss Essie told me there is a no refund policy." Henry always called his stepmother Miss Essie, he would never call her mom.

Right! I thought. *No one in their situation would miss out on a paid camping trip. I never told Henry about Shelly's family business, even though he asked a lot of questions about Laura.*

We were almost to the highway when we heard a lot of honking coming from a white minivan labeled "Bodega Party Store" as it pulled up next to us. The sight was hilarious, with Laura's and Shelly's parents waving and screaming to the driver to pull over on a side street.

Alante had been winning at Rock-Paper-Scissors when he noticed the minivan. "Mr. Borzak, please pull over. It's Shelly and Laura!" he pleaded. Everyone started shouting, "Yeah, let them get on the bus." The noise was so loud, the only thing to do to quiet down the campers was to pull over.

Mr. Borzak shook his head as he grumbled irritably to the bus driver, "Every year this happens. Pull over there Marcus, at the Super Center and let them get on the bus." He added, "And turn that news station off before you scare the kids with all that robbery stuff."

"But sir, I just want to hear the game scores." Mr. Marcus protested.

"Turn it off now! You can't listen to the radio while you're driving anyway," countered Mr. Borzak.

After Mr. Borzak had words with Shelly's and Laura's parents, we were off to the I-83.

Alante, looked relieved, giving the girls high-fives as they took their seats. Timmy picked on Laura about wearing a dress saying, "You don't wear a dress to camp. You look like a prissy little girl!"

Shelly said, "You're a peewee boy with bad jokes and buckteeth. Mind your own business!"

"Hey, are you a boy or a girl?" Jason asked her. "I can't tell with those coke bottle glasses on."

They continued to tell jokes.

"Leave those girls alone!" Mr. Borzak hollered back at them.

"Hey Mr. B; trust me," Henry said, "Shelly and Laura can handle themselves." Henry and I looked at each other and laughed.

"Yes, those clowns will find out once we get to camp." I said.

"It's going to be a fantastic summer!" Henry said, laughing as he settled back into the seat.

I remembered that my mom had bought us journals so we could write about our adventures at camp. I pulled out my journal and started a game of hangman with Henry. After a few games, Henry fell off to sleep and I started to write. It was a long ride.

Finally, we crossed the Susquehanna River. Mr. Borzak talked with me because I was directly across from him.

"Erik, did you know the Susquehanna River is 444 miles long?" he asked me. "The Susquehannock Indian tribe lived in the area where our campground is located." I was looking at him, but I really wasn't paying any attention to the rest of the story. I was imagining what it was like back then to be a Native American boy.

I was a young boy named Riding Star, out hunting with my father, Chief Raging Bull. We hunted for deer and beavers. I had a new bow and arrow. My father had a larger version of my bow on his back and he held a spear in his left hand.

His skin was covered with tattoos that told a story of our tribe's history. He taught me how to track, hunt, and fish all day. We had fun away from the tribe. That's when my father would let his guard down.

As we trailed back to our village, suddenly we were surrounded by our rivals. I heard my father call out, "Riding Star, run!" I dropped everything and ran to get help.

I ran deep into the woods, pursued by two of the rivals. As I glanced back and I saw my father struggling. They had caught him…

Tapping my shoulder, Mr. Borzak brought me out of my daydream. "Erik, look! There's the campground." We had finally arrived. I shook Henry. "Wake up! Wake up! We're here!"

We looked out the window and saw a large totem pole sign that read "Camp Susquehanna."

Everyone on the bus was awake and noisy again with anticipation. We got off the bus, picked up our bags, and listened to the group counselors' directions. They divided the two buses into four bunkhouses. The boys went to bunks at Camp Elm (E-Zhou-U-Ti) and Camp Oak (Tosh-Ka-hi-U-ti). The girls went to bunks at Camp Lake (Ney-a-ti) and Camp Brook (Wa-Shis-Ka-A-ti).

Henry and I were in the E-Zhou-U-Ti. Alante, Timmy, and Jason were in the Tosh-Ka-hi-U-ti. Laura and Shelly were at Ney-a-ti. Most of the kids in the other bunkhouse were not from our neighborhood, but some of the kids were from our school.

We had dinner around the campfire and snacked on peanut butter and chocolate smores. Mr. Borzak told us stories of the land. Then he allowed the camp counselors to share a few ghost stories.

One story I liked, told by group leader Charlie, was about the wandering ghost who captured lost campers in the woods. "So, don't get lost tomorrow!" they whispered spookily at the end.

Alante was a little scared, so he stayed in our bunkhouse that night. We were up late because of all those ghost stories. We told jokes and played around feeling silly about being afraid. It was midnight before we went to sleep. The counselors did bed checks every few hours, so they found my brother in the extra bed next to me and allowed him to stay that night.

After breakfast, all the campers were ready to go hiking. We set off on two different trails. We took the Elk Trail; the other campers took the Moose Trail.

"Our trail goes to the mountains," Henry said. "I can't wait to show off my climbing skills."

The trail was long and it was hot. When we finally stopped for a break near the river, Mr. Borzak allowed us to eat lunch. When Henry, Alante, Laura, Shelly, and I finished eating, we left the others campers and snuck off to sight-see. The area felt so familiar to me, like I had been there before in a dream. We walked for a while, enjoying stories from Shelly and Alante.

"Mr. B will be calling after us. We'd better get back," Henry said.

"Hold on a minute. Did you hear something?" Laura said.

"Is it Mr. Borzak?" I asked.

"No!" she replied, "it was a heavy whispering sound, not Mr. B's high-pitched voice."

"Maybe it's the wandering ghost," Shelly said.

"But we're not lost," Alante said. He looked a bit concerned, like the night before, but then he laughed and said spookily, "The ghost is coming to get you, Shelly."

"Wait, I hear it too," I said.

"Me too Erik; and it's getting closer," Henry added, nervously.

We started heading back to the riverside, back to the other campers. I got this creepy feeling, then out of nowhere, a seven-foot-tall man appeared wearing the coolest buckskin clothing.

We froze!

"Over there!" he said, pointing at the mountains. "Don't go over there!"

Don't go over there!" He repeated it again and again.

Slowly, we looked in the direction that he was pointing, and when we turned back around, the man was gone - but the whispering sound was still there. We took off running down the hill.

"There you guys are!" Mr. Borzak scolded. "We were just coming out to look for you. Don't go off by yourselves next time."

"Mr. B, there was a strange man in the woods," Henry said breathlessly.

"I'm sure it was your imagination. This is a private campground with no public hiking trails. Now, once again, stay close by."

"But we all saw him," said everyone agreeing with Henry.

"Okay, okay, we'll check it out later kids," Mr. Borzak said, but I doubted that he would.

We started hiking toward the path where the spooky man had pointed. We looked suspiciously at the trail we were about to travel.

Laura said, "At least we are with the others now; he can't attack all of us."

"I don't think he wanted to attack us," I said quietly.

We came upon a clearing with a small hill to climb.

"Listen up campers!" group leader Charlie yelled. "We're going to teach all of you the basics of rock climbing and excavation."

"We will teach you in two groups," Mr. Borzak added. "One group will learn about excavation and will go digging while the other half is learning to climb."

They put all of us into the digging group, including Timmy Tautlebaum and Jason Beekman.

"Great!" Shelly said with a frown.

"Oh brother, we're with the prissy girl team!" Timmy said.

Shelly rolled her eyes and walked away with Laura following closely behind. We left the other campers and went left of the mountain, where the counselors told us the soil was much richer for digging.

"Okay team; get out your hand shovels," Mr. Borzak said. "The proper way to dig is to find your site, take your rope and mark it off, then use your hand shovel to carefully remove the top soil. If you find something, use your hands to remove the rest of the soil gently, so you do not damage your find. Go pick your site and good luck!"

We dug for a couple of hours and we found some cool stuff like coins, beads, and broken pots. Nothing great though! When Laura told us to go closer to the mountain, Timmy came over and pushed her. He called her a miss-know-it-all. The next thing we saw was Shelly holding Timmy in a head lock. Jason came over to help and Laura gave him a karate chop across his back and he fell on the ground.

"I told Mr. B that those girls could handle themselves." Henry said chuckling.

"Right! A junior black belt does come in handy," I said. We leaned over together, laughing.

When I looked up, Alante was gone. "Hey guys, where did my brother go?"

"He went over there, closer to the mountain," Laura said while dusting off her clothes.

"Let's go find him," Shelly said.

"Shouldn't we tell Mr. Borzak?" Laura asked.

"Let's find him ourselves," I said. "Besides, he didn't believe us when we told him about the mystery man. He probably thinks we're playing a prank."

We headed off north of the mountain, leaving Timmy and Jason embarrassed at being beaten by girls. They weren't joking around anymore.

We called out to Alante. It was a long time before he answered, his voice echoing from the mountainside.

"Hey guys, over here!" Henry yelled. "Check it out—a cave opening."

We entered and found Alante digging at a site he'd made. I was mad, but happy we found him.

"Alante, don't go off by yourself again!" I said.

"Sorry guys, but look what I found," he said.

We got closer to see what he was doing. There was just a little light shining through the opening of the cave to see.

"Wow," Laura said, "that's neat! You found a wood carving. It looks like a coyote."

Alante removed more dirt and picked up another carving. He wiped off the dirt and showed us. It was a wolf.

"Help me guys," he said. It wasn't long before each of us had dug up an animal carving.

"Look guys, I found a bear!" I exclaimed.

"I have an eagle!" Henry said.

The girls found two owls.

"A horse!" whispered Alante. "Let's not tell anyone about this site. We can come back tomorrow."

We left the cave to meet up with a stern-looking Mr. Borzak. "All of you will have a time-out tomorrow. You will not join us on the Moose Trail for any activities and if you do not listen again; I will inform your parents."

"Sorry Mr. Borzak," we said in unison.

Later that night, we observed the carvings in detail.

"Is it a toy?" Alante asked.

"I think these animals are some kind of necklace worn by the native children, instead of an actual toy, Laura said. "Let me have those; I have an idea,"

We each gave Laura our animal carving and she left. When she returned, it was almost bedtime, and she had the owl tied around her neck.

"I made us necklaces like the native children," she said. She opened her hand and each of us took the carving that we had found and put it around our neck.

"I'll wear the wolf," Alante said. "Let's give mom and dad the horse and coyote as a gift."

Timmy and Jason stood nearby, trying to listen to what we were talking about. *Still sore*, I thought.

The next day was pretty quiet after all of the campers left. We were on the campgrounds with two counselors and the cook as punishment for not following directions.

"Hey Erik," Alante said. "we have to go back to our site before someone else finds it."

"Yeah," Shelly said excitedly, "there could be more cool stuff up there."

"What do you guys think?" I asked Laura and Henry.

"I think we should go. It was our find," said Henry. Laura agreed.

"Okay listen," I said, "this is what we'll do. When we finish swimming, we'll tell the counselors that we're going to go in to change and then get lunch."

We took our last jump in the lake and went ahead with our plan. It wasn't hard to fool the counselors and get away; they were too busy talking to each other. We just laughed as we looked off in their direction and headed toward our bunks to change.

"Hey you guys," Alante called out from his bunkhouse, "the horse and coyote necklaces are gone!"

"I bet it was Timmy and Jason that took them," I said. "Don't worry, we'll get them back."

We left for the Elk Trail. We started in the same direction as we had gone the day before, taking a short break near the river. Alante and I listened to Henry telling us the proper way to climb a mountain. Shelly and Laura went closer to the river's edge to skip rocks.

"Look at this animal carving, guys," I said. "I think Laura was wrong; it's not a necklace. Last night I had that dream again about the Native American boy Riding Star, and you know that tall guy in the woods yesterday? I think that was his father Raging Bull."

"Erik, you're crazy! You're saying that was a ghost?" Henry asked.

"Look at your necklace," I said. "No, really look at it. You see, there's a small hole."

"So what!" Alante said.

"So what?" I said. "As I'm running in my dream, Raging Bull tells me to blow my whistle and call for help. This bear carving is a whistle. I know it sounds crazy you guys, but I swear it's true."

They looked at me like I was an alien for another planet. Then we heard a splash.

"Help! Help!"

We ran to the river's edge where Shelly stood screaming, "Laura fell in the water!"

Laura was beginning to go downstream fast with the current. We kept pace with her, running on the embankment, but she was starting to go under. I saw Laura trying her best to stay above water.

Then my ears almost popped when I heard a loud whistle. Did I hear right? An eagle? A large eagle appeared with a wing span of about eight feet, swooped down and picked Laura up out of the water.

Whoa! Amazing! We all stood there shocked, looking at our animal carvings.

"Erik, you were right!" Henry said, breathlessly. "I believed you and blew into the carving for help. It is a whistle. That eagle appeared right away."

Laura shivered. She was cold from the water.

"So cool!" Henry said, barely able to contain his excitement as he gave Laura his camp shirt to dry off.

"But why is this happening to us?"

As if in answer to Henry's question, the seven-foot tall man appeared – seemingly out of nowhere. He spoke in a low, deep voice.

"Children, do not be afraid. I am here to help you," he said.

"Are you Raging Bull?" I asked hesitantly.

"Maybe," he answered quietly.

"What do you want from us?" I asked.

"Now that you have found and used a communicator, I will tell you what they mean and how to use them."

"Communicator?" Alante asked.

"Yes, he replied. "Communicators—or whistles, as you call them—represent a spiritual creature that will come to life when you blow into its head. It is one with your spirit, and will do as you ask. It is no accident that you found them. It was destiny."

"But Laura almost drowned," Henry said, perplexed. "What if I didn't blow into the whistle?"

"Yeah, why didn't you help her?" Shelly asked, accusingly.

"She would not have drowned," Raging Bull replied quietly. "I have no physical power in the natural world, but I have the power to summon the ancient spirits to help you in a life or death situation. I am your guide, and I must teach each of you how to use your communicator. Now, please blow into your whistles."

We each took a turn blowing into our whistles.

Alante's whistle howled like a pack of wolves.

Henry's whistle gave the call of an eagle.

Laura's and Shelly's whistles sounded like the hooting of owls.

I blew into mine and a great big bear growl came out of it.

"Turn around and see your warriors," Raging Bull said calmly. "You each possess some of the traits of your chosen animal."

We turned and stared in awe. Each animal stood beside us, as if waiting for our instructions. They were majestic and real to the touch. All our fear left us and we bonded with the animals.

The bear showed me strength that could knock over a tree. *Pow!* The tree fell into the water.

"Erik, you have already shown strength and leadership. Your warrior is the bear," Raging Bull said.

The eagle soared high in the sky, swooping down and picking up Henry.

"Son," Raging Bull said to Henry, "you believed in something that you had not seen. Your faith will lead you far. The majestic eagle is your warrior."

The wolf nudged Alante to get on his back and then ran swiftly through the trees.

"Little Alante, the most curious of all. You are quick on your feet. The wolf will be your warrior."

The twin owls dug their large talons in the trees and then climbed quickly to the top.

"The girls are knowledgeable and make good observations – they are the owls."

Just then, we heard footsteps getting closer. The noise of the falling tree had brought the campers back down the trail. Henry said that while he was flying above, he had seen them coming.

"Remember children," Raging Bull cautioned, "do not ever use these creatures for bad deeds."

Then he and the animals vanished.

"Let's go!" I said. We ran back towards camp, where we eased into our bunk houses, pretending we had been there all the time.

PART TWO

Beyond Camp Susquehanna, over where the kids were warned not to venture, lay the hideout of the Hiraqi Bandits. The bandits had committed multiple burglaries throughout the United States. Just when the cops thought they could nab them, they disappeared. A bounty had been placed for their capture. The leader of the Hiraqi Bandits, Rough Rider, had watched the whole scene play out with Raging Bull and the children through his telescopic binoculars.

After the campfire sing-along that night, all of us went off to bed. By the last bed check, I could not get back to sleep. The camp was quiet with the exception of the crickets chirping. Suddenly, the bandits appeared and stole our whistles along with other valuable items.

I followed them to their hideout, a cave past the Elk Trail. I watched the bandits sitting around laughing and talking about all the things they had stolen. I also saw the leader, Rough Rider wearing all the whistles around his neck.

I returned to the campground just as everyone was waking up. When they noticed their belongings were missing; the camp went into an uproar.

"Shouldn't we call the police, Mr. Borzak?" one group leader asked.

"The phone lines have been cut," group leader Charlie said.

"Sounds like those roving Hiraqi bandits have hit us," the bus driver said. "The cops said they always cut the phone lines after their robberies, so they have more time to get away."

"Right!" "They must have known we didn't have cell phones," Charlie said. "They grabbed the two-way radio also."

"Is anyone hurt?" Mr. Borzak called out. All the group leaders, the driver, and the cook counted the children. Everyone was accounted for and no one was hurt.

All of the children were wondering if this was going to be the end of their vacation. Most of the kids were upset and some of the younger children began crying.

"Calm down children," Mr. Borzak said. "I'm going into town to get help. Remain with your group leaders until I return."

I knew exactly where the Hiraqi bandits were hiding; I just needed a plan. *We have to catch the thieves and return all that property*, I thought. *We have to get those whistles!*

The group leaders took us all into the mess hall. The cook gave us breakfast and we sat and talked. As we were talking, along came Timmy and Jason.

"We don't want you guys at our table," Laura said, angrily.

Shelly added, "That's right! Go sit somewhere else!"

"Look guys," Timmy said, "I know we acted rudely the other day. We came to apologize."

We looked at one another and then they held out their hands to display the missing horse and coyote whistles.

"We know your secret," Jason said, handing the whistles to Alante.

"We came to help," Timmy added quietly.

"Why? You could have just kept quiet," Henry said.

"No, those thieves stole my grandfather's stopwatch," said Timmy frowning.

"They took my collection of baseball cards," Jason added nervously nibbling on his lower lip. "They're worth a lot of money, and my mom told me not to bring them."

"Seems like we were punished for taking what didn't belong to us," Timmy said. "Sorry guys."

"Have a seat," I said, making room for them on the bench.

"I think with these two whistles, we can get in the bandits' camp and distract them. We have to get that leader alone."

"But how?" everyone seemed to ask all at once.

"I am still thinking about that one," I said. "I know we can't allow those guys to use our whistles for bad things."

"I have a plan."

"Hey, whale!" Jason said to Danny Wickles. "Did you take all of the sausages? Don't they feed you enough already?" Everyone stopped and stared at the twosome.

Danny was bigger than all of us and he didn't like being called a fat boy. He stood up, towering over Jason.

"I know you're not talking to me," Danny said. "Didn't you get beat up by those girls?"

One of the counselors told them to sit down. Instead, Danny took his chocolate-covered pancakes with whipped cream topping and smashed them in Jason's face.

Led by Timmy, the group started yelling, "Food fight!"

We made our getaway to the woods. The counselors didn't even notice. The plan had worked.

I led Henry, Alante, Shelly, and Laura to the bandits hiding place following the path I had taken earlier.

"Those darn wild dogs!" Bandit One said. He cracked his knuckles when he spoke.

"That does not sound like any dog I've ever heard," Bandit Two said. He was showing off his kick-boxing skills. "I'm gonna kill 'em when I catch up to them."

"It's not dogs, you fools! It's a coyote," Rough Rider replied. He had a long scar on his face and he looked mean. Rough Rider was still checking out the loot they had stolen from the camp.

"I've never seen a coyote out here," Bandit Three said. He was short with a white beard.

"Just because you haven't seen one doesn't mean a thing," Rough Rider said. "Now keep quiet! I need to concentrate. Y'all had better get some rest before we start our big heist tomorrow."

"Yeah boss," Bandit Four said, "If those whistles work like you said, the police will never be able to stop us," he sputtered, laughing as he spoke. He sounded like an evil clown.

The thieves dozed off as the coyote approached the camp. The coyote straddled Rough Rider, and being the trickster that he was, quickly multiplied over each of the bandits. Startled, they woke up staring into the coyotes' snarling faces.

I rode the wild horse into the camp. He took me straight to Rough Rider. I got off the horse, reached down and said, "These are ours!" as I snatched the whistles from around his neck.

"Get 'em, boys!" Rough Rider shouted.

The bandits jumped up and began to fight. Rough Rider grabbed Alante and the Illusion of the multiple coyotes began to fade. I quickly jumped back on the horse and rode to meet my friends. There I gave each of them their whistles.

"Hurry, we have to help Alante," I shouted. They blew their whistles and the great creatures appeared.

Henry flew off with the eagle toward the camp. The Eagle grabbed the bandit and flew him to the mountaintop.

Two of the other bandits were caught by the twin owls that took them high up into the tall trees, where there was nowhere to escape.

The wild horse cornered the last bandit in the cave. The bear covered the opening with a large boulder.

After fighting off the coyote, Rough Rider tried to escape to the river, but was stopped by the call of the wolf.

As he reached the river's edge, the large wolf appeared and backed him up into a trapper's ditch. He fell in and couldn't get out.

The seven-foot tall man in buckskin clothing—Raging Bull—came to us out of a cloud of smoke.

"You did well, my whistle warriors," he said proudly. "That day in the woods, I warned you not to come here, because I thought that you were not ready. But today, my warriors, you have done a great job. You have made the Spirits glad." With that, he disappeared again.

"I can't believe we caught them!" Alante said in disbelief.

"I knew we could do it," Henry said confidently.

"Let's get back before they miss us," Laura said, anxious that we would be in trouble again.

"Too late," Shelly said as she pointed down toward the Elk Trail, "they're already coming."

Mr. Borzak, the police, and all the campers were soon right in front of us.

"Kids! Kids! I'm glad you are all right!" exclaimed Mr. Borzak. "But, you have gone off too many times by yourselves. I'm afraid you will all have to be sent home. Now that our phone service is restored, I'll be calling your parents to come and get you."

"Look there!" Mr. Marcus shouted out. "It's those bandits everyone is looking for."

He was pointing over to the cave opening where all the bandits were tied together, knocked out cold.

"What happened here, kids?" a policeman asked.

We were a little surprised to see the bandits all bundled up together, and not where we had left them. Then I saw Raging Bull smiling at me from near the cave entrance. The animal warriors stood with him. No one could see them but us.

"They caught them. Can't you tell?" Timmy said.

"That's right!" the cook said "Hey, those kids should be given the reward."

Mr. Borzak looked amazed and happy. Everyone cheered for us.

The police went over to the cave, where it took several minutes to wake the bandits. As they handcuffed the crooks, they wondered why the bandits were saying weird things about forest creatures attacking them.

When the police entered the cave, they found all the items that the bandits had stolen, including the items from our cabins.

"Well kids, it sure looks like you are due the reward," the police captain said. "What are you going to do with all that money?"

The others all looked at me.

"We have a friend in need. That money will help her save her house." I said looking at Shelly. Her eyes widened in surprise. She nodded and smiled.

"Good kid, that sounds wonderful."

Later that day, the news broadcasted that a group of local kids had helped save their summer camp from the Hiraqi Bandits. The bandits had been caught and thrown in jail.

We were all thankful to Raging Bull and those great animal warriors. We vowed that we would continue to use our special gifts to always help those in need.

Timmy and Jason were forgiven. They had certainly learned their lesson.

Mr. Borzak decided not to call our parents to come get us.

Wow! I wonder what other adventures await us this summer? I thought.

CPSIA information can be obtained
at www.ICGtesting.com
Printed in the USA
LVIC012252040613
336981LV00002B

9 781481 708296